Othello, the
Moo

Sweet Cherry
Publishing

Published by Sweet Cherry Publishing
53 St. Stephens Road, Leicester, LE2
1GH, United Kingdom

© Macaw Books
Othello, the Moor of Venice

Text & Illustration by Macaw Books
ISBN-978-1-78226-011-0

Printed and Bound by CPI Group (UK) Ltd., Croydon, CR0 4YY

∼⚬⚬✣ About ✣⚬⚬∼
Shakespeare

William Shakespeare, regarded as the greatest writer in the English language, was born in Stratford-upon-Avon in Warwickshire, England (around 23 April 1564). He was the third of eight children born to John and Mary Shakespeare.

Shakespeare was a poet, playwright and dramatist. He is often known as England's national poet and the 'Bard of Avon'. Thirty-eight plays, one hundred and fifty-four sonnets, two long narrative poems and several other poems are attributed to him. Shakespeare's plays have been translated into every major existent language and are performed more often than those of any other playwright.

Othello: He is a general in the Venetian Army. He is a powerful figure, respected by all. He wins the heart of Desdemona because of his  virtues. But later in the play, he kills her because of his insecurities based on racial and cultural differences.

Desdemona: She is the beautiful daughter of Brabantio and wife of Othello. She appears meek, but is determined and confident.

Iago: He is an ensign to Othello and the villain of the play. He is manipulative, cunning, bold and relentless. He is motivated for several reasons to take his revenge on Othello and Cassio.

Cassio: He is second in command to Othello. He is young and good looking, but lacks military experience. Iago resents his position in the military and uses him as a pawn to take revenge on Othello.

Othello, the Moor of Venice

Brabantio was one of the richest senators in Venice. He had a very beautiful daughter called Desdemona, whom all the men of Venice were crazy about.

But Desdemona always preferred the mind over the physical attributes of men – and these qualities could only be fulfilled by a black man called Othello, the Moor of Venice. Othello was very close to Brabantio, and during the many visits he had made to the senator's house, the lovely Desdemona had fallen in love with him.

But though Othello was a black man, the truth remained that there was no other like him in the whole of Venice.

He had proved himself over and over again in the several wars fought between the state of Venice and the Turks. He had established himself as one of the greatest generals the Venetian Army had ever seen, and his strategies of war spoke truly of his intellectual acumen.

But though Brabantio was well aware of the various good qualities of the Moor, he was not willing to have him as his son-in-law. He had always hoped that his daughter would choose a senator or someone of nobler rank, and definitely a white-skinned man like himself. So her choice of

Othello had not gone down very well with him.

When the private marriage between Othello and Desdemona

was made public, Brabantio was convinced that the black Moor had used witchcraft on his poor unsuspecting daughter and tricked her into falling for him.

He declared that it was for this reason that his daughter had not confided in him and had eloped with Othello.

But at that time, there was another important matter that also had to be looked into. News arrived that the Turks

had once again laid siege to the fortress of Cyprus in a bid to take it back from the Venetians. Othello therefore appeared before the senate on two counts – as a general whose services were desperately needed by the state, and also as a fugitive, who had been charged by Senator

Brabantio for having abducted his innocent daughter.

Brabantio's age and seniority in the senate allowed him a hearing from the members of the senate present. But since he was so emotionally charged when making his accusations against Othello, the jury could not take him seriously. On the other hand, Othello merely recounted how he had won over Desdemona by telling her tales of his conquest and other stories whenever he visited Brabantio's house. The court came to the conclusion that

Othello had merely wooed the noble Desdemona and that could not be labelled a crime.

But even more in Othello's favour was the testimony of Desdemona herself. She appeared in court and claimed that while she was indebted to her father for her life and education, she had

chosen to marry Othello of her own accord. The court now had no doubts about the matter and

the verdict was clearly stated in Othello's favour.

Brabantio realised there was nothing he could do but give his daughter to the Moor with his blessing. But in his state of sorrow and misery, he told the Moor, "Look at her, Moor, if you have eyes to see with. She has

deceived her father and she may deceive you as well." So saying, Brabantio left.

Now it was time for Othello to set sail for Cyprus to deal with matters of the state. Desdemona, not wanting to be parted from her husband so soon after their

marriage, asked if she could accompany him. Othello was only too happy to agree. Upon reaching Cyprus, they were told that a tempest had blown away all the Turkish fleets, and so the city was safe from any foreign conquest. Othello was pleased, as now he would have more time to spend with his new bride. Little did he know that the war was just about to begin.

Along with Othello, Michael Cassio had come to Cyprus to face the Turkish invasion. Cassio was one of the Moor's closest friends – a valiant Florentine,

who was adept in charming women off their feet. Any other man would surely be jealous of Cassio being around his beloved,

but Othello felt no jealousy, and had no reason to doubt either Desdemona or Cassio. So, when Desdemona and Cassio spent time together, laughing at Cassio's jokes or at his various stories, Othello did not give it a passing thought.

Othello had recently promoted Cassio to lieutenant, making him second in command. This had not gone down well with many of the soldiers in the army, especially Iago, a more senior officer, who felt that the promotion should have been

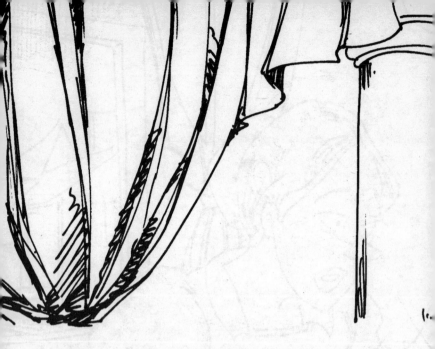

given to him rather than Cassio, a mere novice. It was true that Iago hated Cassio, but now he hated Othello even more.

Iago's wife, Emilia, was a maid to Desdemona and learnt that Othello was madly in love with his wife. Iago then started devising a plan, which would

simultaneously generate the downfall of Cassio, Othello and Desdemona.

Now Iago was a shrewd man and he knew that mental anguish could cause a person much more distress than bodily torture; jealousy was more powerful than the most potent poison. He decided that if only he could prove to Othello that Cassio had been courting his fair wife, it

might be reason enough for Othello to kill Cassio, or vice versa.

With the welcome news of the loss of the Turkish fleet, the whole island of Cyprus was in a state of merriment. Wine was flowing in abundance and everyone drank a toast to Othello and his beautiful wife, Desdemona. It was during that night that Iago decided to put his plan into action. He had met a man called Rodriguez on the island, who was deeply in love with Desdemona and had been heartbroken to learn of her marriage to Othello. Iago knew that this man would perhaps be the best person to help him get things started.

That night, Iago first decided to get Cassio suitably drunk, knowing that he could

not hold his drink. Then, with the connivance of Rodriguez, Iago got him to start talking ill of Bianca, a woman with whom Cassio was very much in love. Cassio, now considerably drunk, soon lost control of his emotions and became embroiled in a fight with Rodriguez. Iago, whom

Othello had put in charge of maintaining peace and order that night, tried to stop them, but only managed to spur them on further.

The ruckus brought Othello out into the streets, and he immediately wanted to know who had started the brawl so that he could mete out an appropriate punishment to the guilty party. But Iago, evil mastermind that he was, tried to place all the blame on himself, declaring to the Moor that it was he who had been unable to stop the fight and so he should be punished. But

finally, when it was learnt that the guilty party was none other than his own lieutenant, Cassio, Othello was beside himself with rage and at once banished him, taking back his title.

Iago kept trying to intervene, begging that Cassio be forgiven,

but Othello was so livid that nothing could change his mind. But in the process, Othello's fondness for Iago grew and he was pleased to see that Iago had a sense of sacrifice.

Later that night, when Cassio rued his actions before Iago, the villain decided to take his game

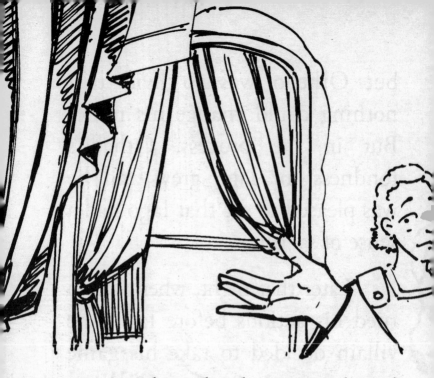

to another level. He advised Cassio that after marriage, wives always have the upper hand over their husbands. He therefore told him to go and plead his case to Desdemona, begging her to help him get back in favour with the general. Cassio, thanking his esteemed friend, decided

to go to meet the noble lady at once. Desdemona was obviously shocked to hear all that had happened that night, and told

Cassio that she would definitely talk to her husband about his case.

When the Moor returned to his wife, she told him that he should immediately forgive Michael Cassio and reinstate

him to his previous rank. Othello tried to delay the topic to a later date, but the innocent Desdemona would not have it. She was adamant that Othello talk to Cassio the next morning and not a minute later. Othello of course did not like this, but to keep Desdemona in good humour, he declared that he would do as she asked.

The next day, Desdemona called Cassio and explained to him what had taken place between her and Othello the night

before, assuring him that he
would soon find favour with the

Moor again. Just as Cassio was leaving after thanking Desdemona for her efforts, Othello and Iago entered the house. Upon seeing Cassio come out of Desdemona's chambers, Iago mumbled, "I do not like that." Othello disliked what Iago was suggesting and immediately asked him the reason for his words. Iago again tried to defuse the situation by diverting the Moor's mind to other matters, but Othello would not give in.

Finally, after many excuses, Iago confessed that he did not enjoy seeing Cassio spend so

much time with Desdemona. After all, the lieutenant was a young man and tales of his charm were well known in Venice. However, he also confirmed that Desdemona was truly in love with her husband and so Othello had nothing to worry about.

Iago knew that he had sown the seeds of jealousy in Othello's mind. All he needed now was some ploy by which to prove to Othello discreetly that Cassio was indeed trying to woo Desdemona, and that his loving wife was actually falling for the young lieutenant. And that chance came rather soon.

Iago's wife, Emilia, went to him a few days later and showed him a handkerchief she had found, wondering if her husband knew to whom it belonged. Now Iago was a rather observant soldier and he at once recognised it as belonging to Desdemona. As a matter of fact, he remembered that it had been a special present from Othello and that she was dearly fond of it. So he put his final plan into action at once.

The next day, when he met Cassio, he tried to cheer him up with tales of how Desdemona would see to it that he was back in favour with the Moor. Cassio also tried to share his enthusiasm and hoped that things would work out for the best. Iago then urged him to spend some time

with his beloved Bianca and
forget about his troubles for a
while. He gave him Desdemona's
handkerchief and told him to
give it to Bianca as a gift, which
would make her love him even
more. Cassio, thinking that
Iago was truly his best friend in

the whole world, thanked him profusely and set off for Bianca's quarters.

Later that day, when Iago was alone with Othello, he tried to talk to him about Cassio. He told Othello that the young man was most honourable and would often give his beloved Bianca gifts. Why, just the other day he had seen him give her a beautiful handkerchief, much like the one the Moor had given Desdemona. This immediately set Othello's mind racing as he wondered how the handkerchief that his friend mentioned could be the same as the one he had given to his wife.

The Moor told Iago of his suspicions, and though Iago tried to dispel his fears at first, he mentioned how Cassio had been showing it off as a gift

from a beautiful lady. This raised Othello's suspicions, and he realised that his fair Desdemona had been seeing Cassio and exchanging love tokens with him. Othello wanted to murder Desdemona immediately, but Iago convinced him to first see if there was any truth in it.

So that night, Othello decided to put the question to Desdemona. Meanwhile, Iago assured Othello that he would arrange Cassio's death and ensure that he never heard of the vile lieutenant again.

When Othello went into Desdemona's room that night,

he pretended to be unwell. He asked for a handkerchief to wipe his brow, and when she gave him her own, he asked her for the one that he had given to her as a gift. She admitted honestly that the handkerchief was lost. But Othello then told her that he knew she had given

it to Cassio as a token of her love. Desdemona was distraught. She could not believe that her husband, the man she loved, was accusing her of being in love with someone else.

Othello was now convinced that Desdemona was feigning ignorance and trying to divert

his attention from the matter at hand. Unable to bear her dishonesty any longer, he suffocated her in bed with a pillow.

Emilia, who as usual had gone to check if her mistress needed anything before she went to sleep, entered the room and was the first to discover the gory murder. She started wailing, which alerted the guards. When they discovered the noble Desdemona dead, they were shocked when they realised the culprit was none other than their general, the valiant Othello.

Othello lost no time in telling them what had happened

over the past few days. He explained how Desdemona had been disloyal to him and that she returned the love of Michael Cassio. He also explained the episode about the handkerchief, but at this point, Emilia entered. She told the people present that she had found the handkerchief and given it to Iago. Othello realised that Iago had been lying

to him about Desdemona the whole time, and it dawned on him that he had murdered his innocent wife simply because he could not keep his jealousy in check. Unable to live with his guilt, Othello drew his sword and slit his own throat, falling over the body of the sweet Desdemona, dead.

Meanwhile, Iago had been able to wound but not kill Cassio, while Cassio had managed to elude the murderous Iago and drag himself, limping, to the court, followed all the way by his murderer. But as soon as Iago entered the room, the guards tried to arrest him. Iago, looking at the people present, knew at once that his wife must have told them the story about the handkerchief. Without wasting another moment, Iago thrust his knife into his wife, killing her almost instantly. But though Emilia could not be saved, the guards arrested Iago at once. Later, he was charged with the murder of all three people – Othello, Desdemona and Emilia – and was sentenced to a most gruesome death. A fitting punishment indeed for the man who had killed the noble Othello and his treasured Desdemona.